FOR KATHRYNE, OSCAR, AND HARVEY.
WITH THANKS TO STEVE AND NIKKI.
—J.C.

TO FINN AND REYNARD
—N.M.

TO DOWNLOAD THE SONG
"MAY THE STARS DRIP DOWN," VISIT
WWW.ABRAMSBOOKS.COM/MAYTHESTARSDRIPDOWN

The artwork was cut and torn from black paper.

Library of Congress Cataloging-in-Publication Data
Chatelain, Jeremy.
May the stars drip down / by Jeremy Chatelain ;
illustrated by Nikki McClure.
pages cm
Summary: A lullaby that invites the reader to take a starlit journey from a wide
desert, down a mountain path, and on to a coastline town.
ISBN 978-1-4197-1024-7
1. Lullabies—Texts. 2. Children's songs, English—United States—Texts.
[1. Lullabies. 2. Songs.] I. McClure, Nikki, illustrator. II. Title.
PZ8.3.C39May 2014
782.421'582—dc23
2013008241

Printed and bound in U.S.A.
10 9 8 7 6 5 4 3 2 1

Abrams Books for Young Readers are available at special discounts when purchased
in quantity for premiums and promotions as well as fundraising or educational
use. Special editions can also be created to specification. For details, contact
specialsales@abramsbooks.com or the address below.

THE ART OF BOOKS SINCE 1949
115 West 18th Street
New York, NY 10011
www.abramsbooks.com

MAY THE STARS DRIP DOWN

By Jeremy Chatelain

Illustrated by Nikki McClure

ABRAMS BOOKS FOR YOUNG READERS

NEW YORK

May the stars drip down light on you,

And you close your eyes to see the moon,

And sleep will pull you through.

May the starlight find you.

Dreams of sand out in some desert wide,

That will blow all day into the night,

And there will come a new dune.

May the sand wash over you.

Up above the floating clouds of white,

In a spray of stars you climb so high,

Where light spills over from the moon.

May the billowed clouds catch you.

Down a mountain path around a lake,

Where moths and crickets chirp and play,

The wind blows grasses green and blue.

May the path gently lead you.

To a coastline town where porch lights blink,

Till the last house slowly falls asleep,

While waves roll in forevermore.

May you walk the sandy shore.

Somewhere out in the old ocean tide,

Where the seaweed and the starfish hide,

You'll float away on waves of blue.

May the warm tides carry you.

Then the morning light comes gently in,

And you wake to sunshine and the wind,

Whose whispers will ring true.

May I always have you.

May I always have you.